McCordsville Elementary
Media Center

GRANDMA
TELLS A STORY

Lois G. Grambling

illustrated by Fred Willingham

🐾 Whispering Coyote
A Charlesbridge Imprint

A **Whispering Coyote** Book
First paperback edition 2002
Text copyright © 2001 by Lois G. Grambling
Illustrations copyright © 2001 by Fred Willingham

Published by Charlesbridge Publishing
85 Main Street
Watertown, MA 02472
(617) 926-0329
www.charlesbridge.com

Library of Congress Cataloging-in-Publication Data
Grambling, Lois G.
Grandma tells a story / Lois Grambling ; illustrated by Fred Willingham.
p. cm.
Summary: A grandmother and grandfather eagerly anticipate the birth of
their first grandchild.
ISBN 1-58089-057-1 (reinforced for library use)
ISBN 1-58089-072-5 (softcover)
[1. Grandparents—Fiction. 2. Birth—Fiction. 3. Babies—Fiction.]
I. Willingham, Fred, ill. II. Title.

Printed in China
(h c) 10 9 8 7 6 5 4 3 2 1
(s c) 10 9 8 7 6 5 4 3 2 1

Illustrations done in mixed media on Caslon mi-teintes
Display type and text type set in Ignatius and 15 pt. Garamond Regular
Separated and manufactured by Regent Publishing Services
Book production and design by *The Kids at Our House*

To Lara, who in 1984 started me writing;
and to Tyler, who in 1987 kept me going; from Grandma
— L.G.G.

To Joyce Pope, who has been one of the biggest fans and supporters
of my book publishing career
— F.W.

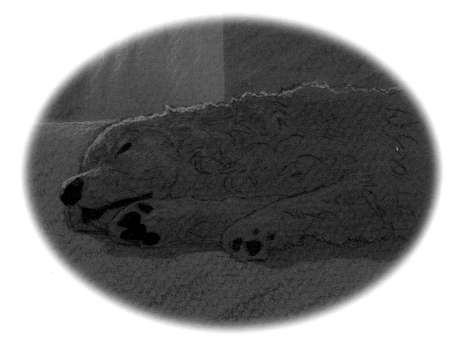

Once upon a time, before you were born, Grandpa and I were very lonely.

We no longer had a child to fill our house with laughter, a child to bake cookies for on a rainy afternoon, a child to read stories to at bedtime.

We had only our dog. And she was getting old.

Each morning when the sun came up we got out
of bed and said to each other, "Wouldn't it be nice if
we had a grandchild to play with today?"

Each night when the moon came up we got into
bed and said to each other, "Wouldn't it be nice if we
had a grandchild to play with tomorrow?"
But we had only our dog. And she was getting old.

Then, one day, a special letter arrived at our house. "You are going to have a grandchild," it said. We were so happy! We danced in the living room. We sang in the bedroom. We hugged our dog—who was sleeping on the kitchen floor.

We opened the window wide. "Listen everyone," we called. "We are going to have a grandchild! Our house will be full of laughter, and it will smell of fresh baked cookies. And we will have someone to read stories to at bedtime."

Now, it takes many months before a grandchild is ready to be born. So we settled down to wait. Week after week we waited. Month after month we waited. Time passed very slowly.

To make the months pass more quickly, we went to town and bought a teddy bear and a book of nursery rhymes.

We went to town again and bought a tiny sweater and a pair of tiny booties.

And still we waited. Then one morning, very early, the phone rang at our house. "You have a grandchild. A wonderful grandchild. The most wonderful grandchild in the whole world."

Grandpa and I were so happy. We danced in the living room. We sang in the bedroom. We hugged our dog—who was sleeping on the kitchen floor.

We opened the window wide. "Listen everyone," we called. "We have a grandchild! A wonderful grandchild. The most wonderful grandchild in the whole world."

The next day, Grandpa got up early and packed the car. In went the teddy bear and the book of nursery rhymes. In went the tiny sweater and the pair of tiny booties. In went the suitcases. In I went, too. (The dog was already sleeping on the backseat.)

We opened the car windows wide. "Listen everyone,"
we called. "We're going to visit our new grandchild."
And Grandpa drove the car merrily down the highway.
Grandpa drove up one hill and down another.
We heard roosters crowing. We saw cows grazing.

Grandpa drove into big cities and out of big cities.
We heard taxis honking. We saw people scurrying.

We have
a new baby!

Then Grandpa drove down one special street
and stopped in front of one special house.

"We are here, everyone," we called. "We are here to play with, and bake cookies for, and read stories to our wonderful grandchild. The most wonderful grandchild in the whole world."

And with arms overflowing with gifts and hearts overflowing with happiness, we hurried into the house.

Grandma and Grandpa are not lonely anymore.

The End.
(But really, just the beginning.)

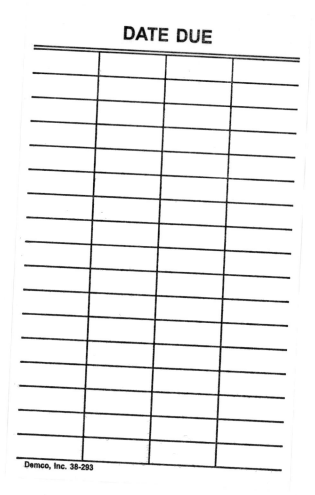

DATE DUE

Demco, Inc. 38-293